ISBN 978-1-84135-785-0

Adapted by Jane Carruth
Illustrated by Rene Cloke

This edition first published 2010

Published by Award Publications Limited,
The Old Riding School, The Welbeck Estate,
Worksop, Nottinghamshire, S80 3LR

10 1

Printed in China

The Wind in the Willows

In the Wild Wood

From Kenneth Grahame's Classic Stories

Award Publications Limited

There were times, after a day spent happily on the river, when Ratty would talk to Mole about his friends, especially Toad and Badger.

"I know Mr Toad, of course," Mole said, as they talked one evening, "but I don't know Mr Badger…"

"Badger lives in the Wild Wood," Ratty explained. "And we certainly don't want to go visiting him there!"

But Mole wanted so very much to meet
Badger and so one morning, when Ratty
had gone fishing, he set out by himself for
the Wild Wood.

It was a cold and wintry day and Mole,
in high spirits, was glad of his warm scarf.
Once in the wood, however, his spirits soon
fell, for it seemed that everywhere he looked
there were little pointed faces watching him.
Suddenly a rabbit sped past, muttering,
"Danger, danger, everywhere! Turn back!"

"What danger could there be?" Mole
asked himself, at once very much afraid.

Meanwhile Ratty had come home. At first he did not worry about his friend, but as the day wore on he grew anxious.

"Wherever can Mole be?" he asked himself over and over again.

It was only when he went to look outside that he spotted Mole's tracks.

"I do believe he has gone to explore the Wild Wood after all!" he exclaimed in dismay. "What a foolish Mole he is!"

Ratty was much too stout-hearted to desert his friend. He went back into the house, put on his warmest clothes and took a stick from his broom cupboard. Then he set off, following Mole's footprints.

When he reached the Wild Wood, Ratty began his search. Along the twisting paths he tramped, calling in a soft voice, "Moley, Moley, where are you?"

Now and then Ratty caught glimpses of sharp little eyes peering at him from behind trees, but he kept on bravely. At last, after an hour's search, he heard a feeble little cry, "Is that you, Ratty? I'm over here!"

The voice came from a hollow at the foot of a tree. Ratty bent down and looked inside. There was Mole, shivering and shaking and looking so scared that Ratty said, "Now pull yourself together, Mole. We must get going to Badger's house at once."

"I'm sorry, Ratty," Mole whispered, "I can't go yet … I'm so tired … and now that you've found me … I feel like a little sleep." And to Ratty's dismay he laid down his head and began to snore.

When Mole awoke it was snowing heavily, and the path through the wood was hard to follow.

As they trudged on through the snow, poor Mole suddenly tripped and fell.

"Ouch!" he exclaimed. "My leg hurts!"

As he comforted his injured friend, Ratty saw what it was that had tripped Mole. Hidden in the snow was a boot scraper!

"Hooray!" shouted Ratty, as be began to dig in the snow. Mole could not understand why Ratty should get so excited about a boot scraper, but then his friend explained. "Badger's house must be buried beneath this snow drift!"

Mole joined in with the digging and presently they came upon first a doormat and then a solid little green door and beside it a brass plate which read 'MR BADGER'.

"You ring the bell pull, Mole" Ratty said, "and I'll knock on the door."

So Mole swung on the bell pull while Ratty hammered on the door, *RAT-TAT-TAT*. After a time they heard a shuffling sound behind the door, then the noise of a bolt being drawn back. The door opened and there was old Mr Badger.

"Do let us in, please, Badger," Ratty cried. "We're lost, and it's so very cold out here."

"Why, Ratty!" exclaimed Badger, in a deep, kindly voice. "Whatever are you doing out in the Wild Wood at night? Come in!"

Badger found them
both dressing gowns and
slippers and sat the friends
down at the kitchen table,
which he laid with plates of delicious food.

"I made the sausage rolls myself this very
afternoon," said Badger, "and there are
plenty of apples and a very tasty vegetable
pie, though I do say so myself!"

Ratty and Mole looked at each other and
smiled. The dangers of the Wild Wood now
seemed miles away.

Over a really wonderful supper, Ratty
told Mr Badger about how he had met
Mole. And then Mole told Badger how he
had come to be in the Wild Wood. "I was
looking for you," he said, smiling.

The three friends talked late into the
night. It was too dark for them to find their
way home, so Badger invited Mole and
Ratty to stay in his spare room.

After the excitement of the Wild Wood,
Ratty and Mole slept very well indeed, and
at breakfast they both had good appetites.
They shared the meal with two young
hedgehogs who had called to see
Badger, knowing he would
give them a fine breakfast.

Then Otter arrived too.
"So there you both are!"
he cried, bursting into
the room. "I tell you, we
were all worried about
you. Some of us searched
by the river bank,
but I thought you
might be here."

Once the two hedgehogs had gone home, Mr Badger invited Mole, Ratty and Otter to stay for lunch.

Lunch was very enjoyable and Mole was so clearly pleased at being with Mr Badger that the kindly fellow offered to show Mole around his house. Mole was delighted, and his new friend lit a lantern and gave him a guided tour through the long dark passages and down the steep walkways, which led into more well-stocked storerooms than Mole could count.

By the time the tour was over, Ratty was impatient to be off. "We don't want to be spending another night in the Wild Wood," he said. "Come on, Moley, get your coat on. You can visit Mr Badger again another time."

"I'm coming too," said Otter. "I know my way around the wood, so I'll lead the way!"

Not long after their adventure in the Wild Wood, the weather changed and the snow disappeared. Mole had been staying with Ratty for so long now that he scarcely ever thought of his own home.

There were so many pleasant and exciting things to do that Mole had very little time to himself to think about his old life.

But all this was to change one day when he was out with Ratty. They had been for a very long walk and had gone much further than usual. "You know," said Mole, stopping suddenly in his tracks, "there is something very familiar about this place. I seem to have been here before." And he sniffed the air. But Ratty paid no attention and strode onwards, anxious to get home.

Mole trotted after his friend. His little face wore such an anxious, troubled look that Ratty couldn't help noticing it when at last they stopped.

"Sit down here," he said in a kindly way, "and tell me what is wrong."

"It-it's just that something about that place reminded me of home," Mole whispered, beginning to sob. "But you wouldn't stop."

"Well now," said Ratty, "what a poor friend you must take me for! I'm afraid I was thinking too much about our supper. Cheer up, Mole, we'll turn back at once!" And he took Mole's paw.

Mole brightened up as they hurried along. Then he began to sniff the air and look about with great excitement.

"What is it, Moley?" Ratty asked at last. "Where are we going?"

"Home!" gasped Mole, his little eyes shining brightly. "I do believe I've stumbled on my old home – my own dear home!"

He had scarcely stopped speaking when
he took a dive through a hedge. Ratty
scrambled through after him and was just in
time to see Mole dart into a tunnel. Inside,
the tunnel had an unfamiliar earthy smell
and was very dark. But Ratty could just see
that at the end of the tunnel it opened out
into a sort of underground chamber.

Mole took a lantern from a nail in the
wall and struck a match to light it. There it
was – the front door of his own house!

"Here we are," said Mole. "We're home!"

Once they were inside, Ratty couldn't help thinking how cold it was, but he said nothing of it. Instead he busied himself collecting bits of wood to make a fire.

Mole became a little downhearted when he saw how damp and dusty his house had become while he had been staying with Ratty, but when he saw the roaring fire that his friend had made he began to cheer up.

He found a duster and set about cleaning the table and chairs. "I-I had forgotten how long I have been away," he said as he dusted. "I was always so proud of my little home. I kept everything neat and tidy."

"I can see that!" Ratty said kindly. "We'll have this place shipshape in no time at all."

"Of course we will!" said Mole.

But Mole's happy mood didn't last for long. When his tummy began to rumble, he suddenly exclaimed, "Oh, dear! There won't be anything in the larder for supper!"

"Come on, Moley," said Ratty, who was also feeling hungry by now. "Let's explore the cupboards. You never know!"

Mole was delighted to find quite a few things to eat. There were delicious sausages and tins of tasty sardines, which they ate with crackers. And they washed it all down with bottles of fizzy ginger pop.

They had just finished their second tin of sardines when they heard the scuffling of small feet outside the front door.

"We've got visitors!" Mole exclaimed. And then came the sound of singing. "I think it must be the carol singers. They would always to come to my house last of all and I would give them hot drinks."

"Let's invite them all in!" Ratty cried, and he ran to the door.

The field mice carol singers made a merry sight as they trooped in and formed a circle and then began to sing tunefully in their squeaky little voices.

But Mole didn't seem to enjoy the lovely carols. "Ratty," he whispered at last. "I'm so worried. They will all be hungry, but we haven't a thing left to give them…"

Ratty said not to worry, and presently he took one of the mice aside while the rest sang on. "Be a good lad," he said in a low voice. "Take this money and buy as many things to eat and drink as you can carry. Fill this basket and come straight back."

"There's a shop in the village which stays open all hours," said the field mouse. "I'll be as quick as I can, sir!" And he hurried off, swinging the basket as he went.

After the mice had sung one or two of
Ratty's favourite carols, he invited them all
to sit on Mole's long bench. It was a tight
squeeze, and there was much pushing and
giggling.

There was still just enough ginger pop
left to fill all their mugs, and as they drank
the mice looked like they were enjoying
themselves greatly. When Ratty invited each
of them to recite their favourite poem, they
all jumped at the chance.

Before too long, the mouse returned
from the village shop, staggering under the
weight of the bulging basket. Mole's eyes
nearly popped out of his head when he saw
all the goodies spread out on the table. It
was a splendid sight indeed.

What a feast they all had! But all too soon it was time for the happy little mice to go home.

Mole and Ratty stood in the doorway to wave them goodbye.

"Goodbye, goodbye!" they called back. "And thank you again!"

Mole sighed with happiness. "It's all thanks to you, Ratty."

The house felt strangely quiet after the carol singers had gone, but Mole didn't mind. He sat with Ratty before the fire, feeling very content with life.

Ratty understood what Mole was thinking. "It's like this, old fellow," he said. "East, west, home is best!"

"How true," said Mole. "But I don't think I want to live here by myself all the time. If you don't mind, Ratty, I'd just like to come home from time to time."

"That's settled then," said Ratty, as Mole rummaged about looking for extra bedding for his friend. "You can come home with me tomorrow, and you'll come back here whenever you feel like it."

Mole nodded happily as he climbed into bed. How well the day had turned out after all. And what a wonderful friend Ratty was! And Ratty, as he closed his eyes, was thinking much the same about Mole.

Soon there wasn't a sound to be heard except for Mole's soft little snuffling snores.